LIFE CAN BE ROUGH.
IT CAN GET TO A POINT WHERE IT SEEMS LIKE EVERYTHING IS CRASHING DOWN AROUND YOUR EARS.
SOMETIMES YOU FEEL THAT WAY EVEN WHEN THINGS ARE GOING SMOOTHLY.
THAT'S WHEN YOU NEED TO ESCAPE, NEED TO GET LOST IN A CROWD.
BY THE WAY, MY NAME'S HANK MCCOY. SOME FOLKS CALL ME THE BEAST.
JACKSON-GUICE

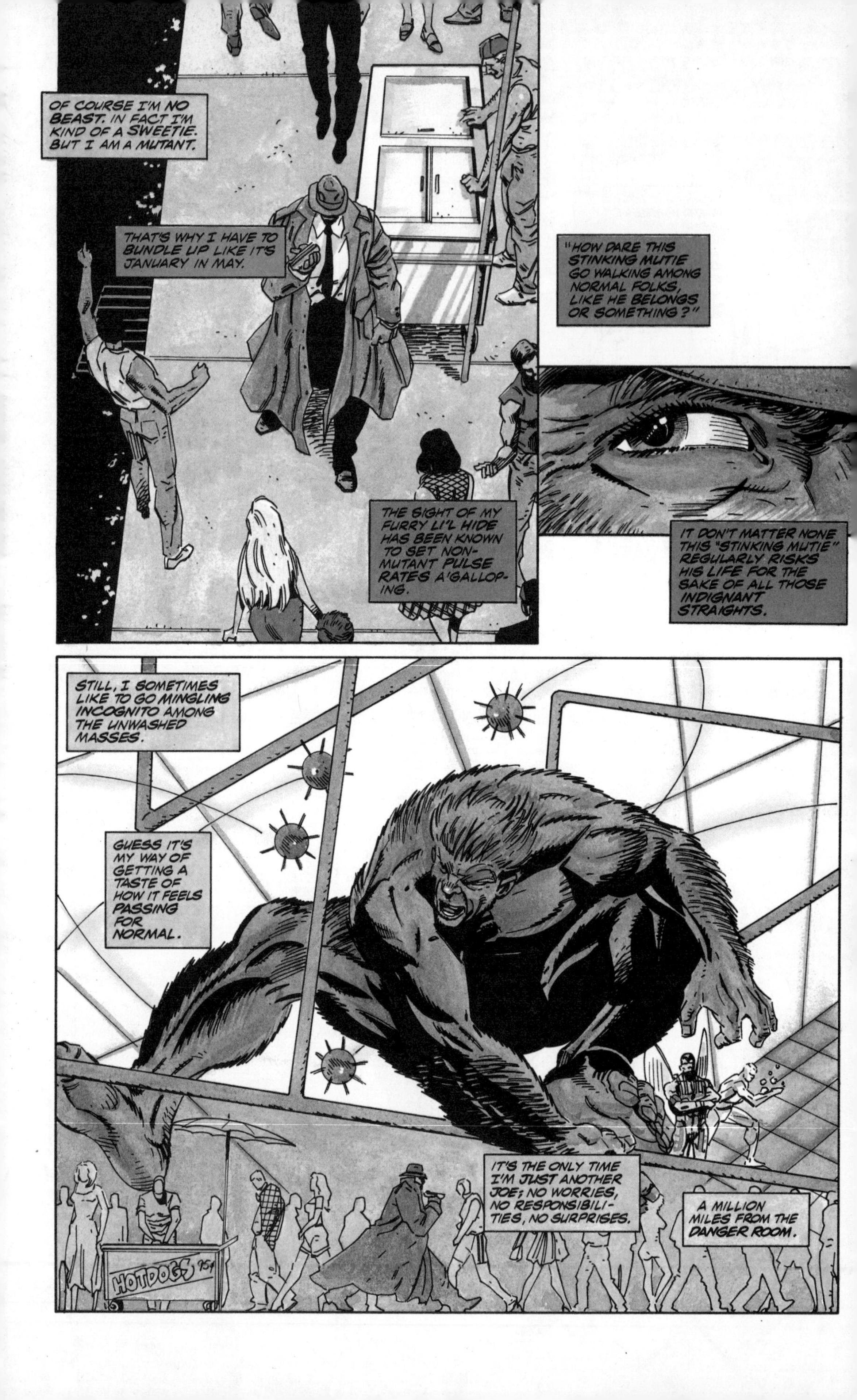
OF COURSE I'M NO BEAST. IN FACT I'M KIND OF A SWEETIE. BUT I AM A MUTANT.
THAT'S WHY I HAVE TO BUNDLE UP LIKE IT'S JANUARY IN MAY.
THE SIGHT OF MY FURRY LI'L HIDE HAS BEEN KNOWN TO SET NON-MUTANT PULSE RATES A'GALLOPING.
"HOW DARE THIS STINKING MUTIE GO WALKING AMONG NORMAL FOLKS, LIKE HE BELONGS OR SOMETHING?"
IT DON'T MATTER NONE THIS "STINKING MUTIE" REGULARLY RISKS HIS LIFE FOR THE SAKE OF ALL THOSE INDIGNANT STRAIGHTS.
STILL, I SOMETIMES LIKE TO GO MINGLING INCOGNITO AMONG THE UNWASHED MASSES.
GUESS IT'S MY WAY OF GETTING A TASTE OF HOW IT FEELS PASSING FOR NORMAL.
IT'S THE ONLY TIME I'M JUST ANOTHER JOE; NO WORRIES, NO RESPONSIBILITIES, NO SURPRISES.
A MILLION MILES FROM THE DANGER ROOM.
HOTDOGS 95¢

THERE, YOU NEVER KNOW WHAT TO EXPECT.
AND I HATE GETTING HIT IN THE FACE WITH A SNOWBALL, ESPECIALLY WHEN IT HAPPENS WITHOUT ANY WARNING.
AACCKK!!
AND AT TWENTY FEET ABOVE THE FLOOR, IT PLAYS HAVOC WITH THE OL' TAILBONE.
KA-THUUDD!!
BOBBY, MY MAN, A FRIEND WOULD HAVE INFORMED ME HE WAS PART OF THIS TEST RUN.

BUT, HANK, THAT'D BE CHEATING.
AND A REAL PAL WOULDN'T ASK SUCH A THING OF A FRIEND.
TELL THAT TO MY ACHING DERRIÉRE, WARREN.
WANT TO GIVE IT ANOTHER TRY?
NO, I'LL PASS.
DON'T SEEM TO HAVE ALL MY CYLINDERS FIRING TODAY.

IN OUR LINE OF WORK, THAT'S A GOOD WAY TO END UP DEAD.
PLEASE, NO SERMONS.
I GET ENOUGH OF THEM FROM SCOTT.

IT'S JUST THAT SOMETIMES A BODY GETS TIRED, LOSES THE EDGE.
AFTER ALL, I'M ONLY HUMAN...

...SORT OF.

I KNOW, BOBBY AND WARREN MEANT WELL. BUT THERE ARE TIMES WHEN YOU JUST DON'T WANT TO HEAR TOO MUCH TRUTH.
SCOTT'S KID, GOING AT IT AGAIN.
YOU NEED TO EAT ALL YOUR PABLUM.
OTHERWISE YOU WON'T GROW UP BIG AND STRONG, LIKE YOUR DADDY.
JUST A LITTLE BIT MORE, CHRISTOPHER.

SPLOOOT!!

CHRIS-1.
JEAN-0.

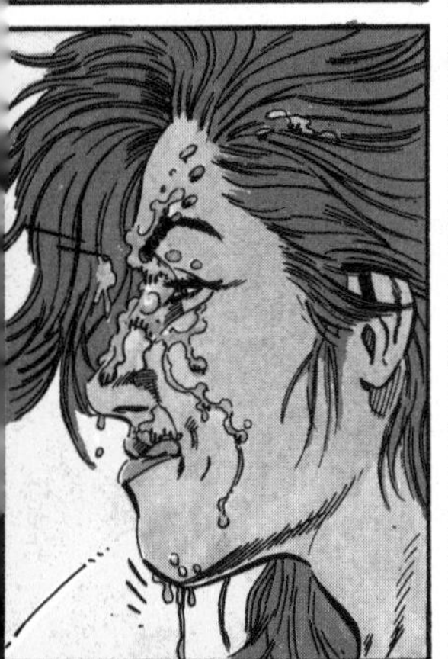

WAAAA!!

THERE, THERE, *BIG FELLA*. IT'S ALL RIGHT.
NO HARM DONE.

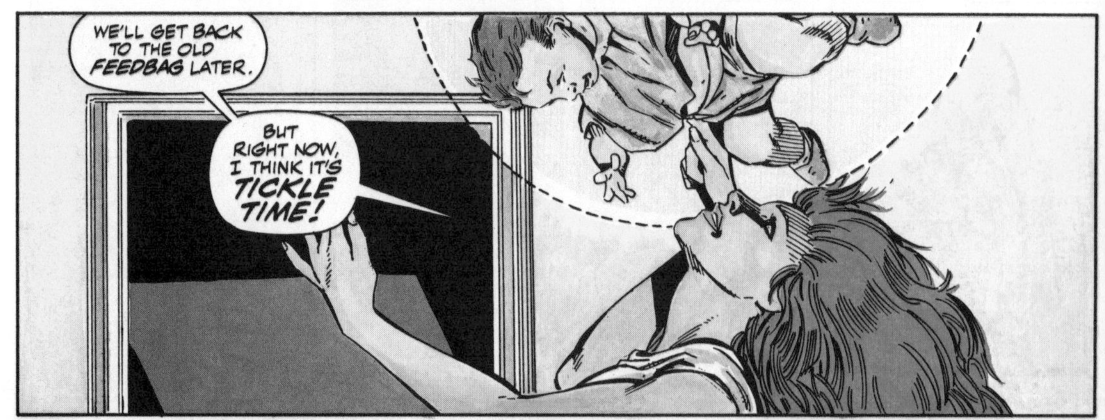
WE'LL GET BACK TO THE OLD FEEDBAG LATER.
BUT RIGHT NOW, I THINK IT'S TICKLE TIME!

BABIES.
WHAT YOU FIGURE THE CHANCES ARE OF YOU EVER HAVING ONE, McCOY?
NEXT TO ZILCH.

AND IF YOU DID HAVE ONE, WHAT WOULD IT LOOK LIKE?
IT MIGHT TAKE AFTER ITS FATHER.

THAT WOULD MAKE FOR A DELIGHTFUL CHILDHOOD. JUST IMAGINE ALL THE MARVELOUS NICKNAMES HE'D HAVE TO GROW UP WITH.
MORNING, HANK.
IS IT?

WHERE YOU HEADING?
OUT.
JUST OUT.

HANK, YOU O.K.?
SURE, SURE. WHY WOULDN'T I BE?

YOU CAN NEVER BE TOO RICH OR TOO SLIM.
C'MON, HANK, SOMETHING IS BOTHERING YOU.

JUST LIFE IN GENERAL.
CATCH YOU LATER.
HEY, IF ANYONE'S GOT THE RIGHT TO OCCASIONALLY HAVE A SNIT, IT'S ME.

I'M A CUTE LI'L FURRY FREAK WHOSE ONLY FRIENDS ARE OTHER FREAKS.
OF COURSE ALL OF THEM CAN PASS AS HUMAN, WHEN THEY LIKE.

IS IT ANY WONDER I SOMETIMES GET THE BLUES?
THAT WASN'T MEANT TO BE A PUN.

LUCKILY I KNOW ONE SURE-FIRE CURE FOR THE BLUES.
GO TAKE A WALK IN THE BIG APPLE.

NEW YORK CITY: THEY SAY IT'S THE GREATEST TOWN IN THE WORLD.
COURSE, SOME MIGHT ARGUE THE POINT.

ALL I KNOW FOR SURE IS THAT IT'S A TERRIFIC PLACE TO GET LOST IN ORDER TO SORT THINGS OUT.
I ALWAYS MANAGE TO PROPERLY REALIGN MY ATTITUDE ON THESE LITTLE STROLLS.

THEY CALL IT A MELTING POT.
I WALK THESE STREETS AND I CAN ALMOST SEE THE DAY WHEN A MUTANT'LL BE ABLE TO GO AMONG THESE FOLKS WITHOUT HAVING A LYNCH MOB COME AFTER HIM.
COURSE, TODAY'S NOT THE DAY, SO I KEEP MY HAT PULLED LOW.

YES, SIR. NEW YORK'S A CITY OF EXTREMES.

IF IT EXISTS, YOU'LL FIND IT HERE.

BUT IT'S GOT TO BE A STRANGE PLACE TO GROW UP IN.

THE TOWN'S CONFUSING ENOUGH LIVING HERE AS AN ADULT, LET ALONE...

THERE SHE GOES DOWN THE ALLEY!
GET HER!!
HUH?

NOW THERE GOES TROUBLE, IF I EVER SAW IT.
IT'S PARTY TIME!

TAKING TO THE HIGH GROUND MIGHT BE A GOOD IDEA.

BEST TO KNOW EXACTLY WHAT'S GOING ON BEFORE COMMITTING YOURSELF TO ANY ACTION.

WOULDN'T I FEEL SILLY IF ALL THAT WAS GOING ON WAS SOME TEEN-AGER TRYING TO CATCH UP WITH HIS GIRLFRIEND.

BUT FOR SOME REASON, I DON'T THINK THAT'S THE CASE.

GENTLEMEN CALLERS DON'T USUALLY COME AROUND CARRYING CROWBARS AND CHAINS.
WE'VE BEEN LOOKIN' FOR YOU, LADY!
JOEY TOLD US WHAT YA DID TO HIS BROTHER!
NO ONE TREATS A RATTLER LIKE THAT!

YER GONNA HAVE TA PAY FER THAT, LADY!

YER GONNA HAVE TO PAY IN BLOOD!

WHUUMPH!

NO ONE'S GOING TO DO ANY BLEEDING AROUND HERE TODAY, CHUMS.
SO WHY DON'T ALL YOU LITTLE PSYCHOPATHS GO HOME AND WATCH SOME BOOB TUBE.
COOL OUT!
DON'T WORRY, MISS.
I'VE GOT EVERYTHING UNDER...
UNDER...
UNDER...
ONE GLANCE AND I'M LOST. I'VE NEVER SEEN ANY-ONE OR ANYTHING SO BEAUTIFUL IN MY WHOLE LIFE.
IT'S PRETTY APPARENT, THE DASTARDLY CRIME SHE COMMIT-TED AGAINST JOEY'S BROTHER.
SHE OBVIOUSLY BROKE THE POOR KID'S HEART...

...AND ALMOST GETS A 5 INCH BLADE DRIVEN INTO MINE.
I DECIDE IT'D BE BEST IF I KEEP MY MIND ON THE PROBLEM AT HAND.
TIME ENOUGH FOR ROMANCE LATER.
THEY REALLY AREN'T MUCH OF A THREAT, JUST A BUNCH OF STREET TOUGHS FLEXING THEIR MUSCLES.
I'LL BE ABLE TO HANDLE THEM WITHOUT BREAKING A SWEAT.

AFTER ALL, I'VE BEEN TRAINED TO TAKE ON SUPER VILLAINS, REAL EARTH SHAKERS.
THIS GROUP IS NOTHING BUT A BAND OF SNOT-NOSED KIDS, HEADING FOR TROUBLE.
SO I GO EASY ON THEM, DON'T REALLY TURN UP THE JUICE.
I MEAN, YOU DON'T USE AN ELEPHANT GUN TO SOLVE AN ANT PROBLEM.
BUT THEN AGAIN...
KA-CHUNK!

GOOD EYE, SHANK!
HE'S A FREAKING MUTIE, THAT'S WHAT!
WHAT'S WITH THIS DUDE?

WHAT WE DO WITH HIM?
I SAY WE WASTE HIM!

NEXT TIME... DEFINITELY USE... AN ELEPHANT GUN...

SAY WHAT?!
WHERE AM I?
IN MY APARTMENT.
AND YOU'RE...?
SYNTHIA NAIP.
DID YOU CARRY ME HERE OR WAS I CAPABLE OF WALKING?
DO I LOOK LIKE I COULD CARRY YOU?
GUESS NOT.
I WANT TO THANK YOU FOR YOUR HELP BACK IN THE ALLEY.
SURE, NO PROBLEM.
SAY! WHAT HAPPENED AFTER I HIT THE CANVAS?
THOSE PUNKS GIVE YOU ANY MORE TROUBLE?

NOTHING I COULDN'T HANDLE.
YOU KNOW YOU SURPRISED ME SHOWING UP THE WAY YOU DID.
I HAD NO IDEA YOU WERE ON THE ROOF.
WELL, WE MUTANTS HAVE A TALENT FOR SHOWING UP JUST IN THE NICK OF TIME.
A MUTANT?
IS THAT WHAT YOU ARE?
MUTANT, MUTIE, HOMO-SUPERIOR...
FOLKS HAVE A LOT OF COLORFUL NAMES FOR MY KIND.
INTERESTING...
GUESS YOU HAVEN'T LIVED HERE LONG?
RELATIVELY SPEAKING, NO.
I'M A STRANGER TO THIS... TOWN.

IN MANY WAYS I AM AS LONELY AS YOU.
WHAT WOULD YOU KNOW ABOUT ME BEING LONELY?
THERE'S A LOT I KNOW ABOUT YOU, HANK McCOY.
YOU KNOW MY NAME?
HOW?
CAN'T YOU FEEL IT, HANK, FEEL IT DEEP IN YOUR HEART?
OUR SOULS HAVE TOUCHED AND FOUND A KINDRED SPIRIT IN EACH OTHER.
I REALIZED THAT THE FIRST MOMENT OUR EYES MET.
EYES? YES... EYES...
I AM THE WOMAN YOU'VE SEARCHED FOR ALL YOUR LIFE.
I AM THE LOVING HEART THAT WILL DRIVE OFF THE DANK AND LONELY NIGHT.
WHAT I SAY IS TRUE, IS IT NOT?
EVERY WORD.
AND YOU ARE JUST WHAT I MOST NEED.
STRONG ARMS TO HOLD ME.
SOMEONE TO WATCH OVER ME.
A PROTECTOR.

SYNTHIA?
ALONE?

SYNTHIA?
SUCH AN EMPTY PLACE.

SPEAKING OF EMPTY, SOME FOOD DOESN'T SOUND LIKE A BAD IDEA.

BUT WHEN HE GOT THERE THE CUPBOARD WAS BARE.
TOO BAD, LI'L BLUE RIDING HOOD.
THE FRIDGE IS IN THE SAME SORRY STATE.
MAYBE THERE'S A DINER SOMEWHERE IN THE NEIGHBOR-HOOD.
THERE IS, BUT WHO NEEDS IT.
I'VE ALREADY FIXED YOU BREAKFAST.

I MADE YOU A DOUBLE HELPING OF EVERYTHING.
SIT DOWN AND DIG IN.
YOU NEED TO KEEP UP YOUR STRENGTH.
HUH... SURE...
SAY, WHERE ARE YOU FROM, SYNTHIA?
FAR FROM HERE.
BEING ENIGMATIC, ARE WE?
NO, IT'S JUST RATHER HARD TO PRO-NOUNCE.

BESIDES, WHAT DOES IT MATTER WHERE I COME FROM?
IT DOESN'T, I GUESS.
ALL THAT'S IMPORTANT IS HOW WE FEEL FOR EACH OTHER.
FEELINGS ARE ALL THAT COUNT.
STAY BY MY SIDE, HANK McCOY.
I'LL TAKE YOU PLACES YOU NEVER DREAMT EXISTED.
TOGETHER WE'LL EXPLORE REALMS BEYOND THE REACH OF YOUR IMAGINATION.
YOU... YOU COULD DO THAT, COULDN'T YOU?
THERE'S NO END TO THE PLEASURE I COULD GIVE YOU.
AND ALL I ASK IN RETURN IS YOUR PROTECTION.
I'D NEVER LET ANYONE HARM YOU.
I KNOW.
HUH?

YOU... YOU BROKE THE SKIN!
DID IT HURT...
...TERRIBLY?
NO...
...NOT AT ALL.
BLOOD RED.

THAT'S WHAT COLOR THE SKY IS.
BLOOD RED.

THE MONSTER'S THE STUFF OF OPIUM DREAMS.
A SLITHERING NIGHTMARE.

HE LOOKS HUMAN, BUT I DON'T BUY THE LIE.
POST NO BILLS
THE DARK ONE RADIATES A BLACK AND OMINOUS POWER THAT CHILLS ME TO THE BONE.
59 St-Columbus Circle Station
A C K B D
HE STRIDES OFF, A SINISTER PURPOSE IN HIS GAIT.
HIS EYES ARE CONSTANTLY IN MOTION, SEARCHING FOR SOMETHING.

OR SOMEONE.
PITY THE POOR SOUL HE SEEKS.
THEN IN A FLASH OF PURE HORROR I REALIZE THE PERSON HE'S HUNTING IS...
SYNTHIA!
SYNTHIA...
THANK GOD...

I HAD A DREAM...
THERE WAS THIS THING... THAT TURNED INTO A MAN...
...AND HE'S COMING FOR ME.
YOU KNOW?
I KNOW ABOUT DREAMS.
YES, IT WAS JUST...A DREAM.
THEN WHY ARE YOU SO SAD, SYNTHIA?
BECAUSE I KNOW TOO MUCH.
I KNOW IT'S A HARSH WORLD OUT THERE...
...WITH SO FEW HAPPY ENDINGS.

YOU'VE BECOME THE WHOLE WORLD TO ME, SYNTHIA, EVEN THOUGH I KNOW SO LITTLE ABOUT YOU.
WHAT ARE YOU, MY LOVE?
ANYTHING YOU WISH ME TO BE.
YOU DO SUCH... STRANGE AND WONDROUS THINGS TO ME.
NOTHING YOU DON'T WANT ME TO DO.

YOU'RE NOT COMPLETELY HUMAN, ARE YOU?
NO.
BUT THEN NEITHER ARE YOU.

NO HUMAN COULD MAKE YOU FEEL THE WAY I DO!
NO HUMAN WOULD WANT TO!
SYNTHIA...

WAIT! DON'T BE ANGRY!
I DIDN'T MEAN TO...

I DON'T KNOW WHAT I MEANT.
I'M SORRY, I'M SO SORRY...

DON'T BE.
YOU CAN'T HELP WHAT YOU ARE... WHAT YOU DON'T UNDER-STAND...

BUT I MIGHT UNDERSTAND IF YOU'D ONLY TALK TO ME.
PLEASE, TELL ME WHAT'S GOING ON HERE.

PERHAPS LATER.

FOR NOW, LET'S CALL IT A NIGHT.

THE MORNING LIGHT BEGINS TO BURN SOME OF THE COBWEBS FROM MY PSYCHE.
E 62
WHAT HAVE I BEEN DOING? I DON'T EVEN KNOW EXACTLY WHERE I AM.
HOW LONG HAVE I BEEN HERE? ONE? TWO DAYS?
SCOTT AND THE GANG WILL BE WONDERING WHAT'S BECOME OF ME, WORRYING.
I'LL HAVE TO GIVE THEM A RING.
BUT SYNTHIA DOESN'T HAVE A PHONE; DOESN'T SEEM TO NEED ONE; APPAR-ENTLY DOESN'T WORK.
I'LL TAKE HER OUT FOR BREAK-FAST THIS MORNING, FIND A PAY PHONE.
MAYBE I OUGHT TO MAKE THAT LUNCH. OR EVEN DINNER.
FEEL SO WEAK. ALL MY MUSCLES HAVE TURNED TO RUBBER.
I'VE NEVER FELT SO WRETCHED. MAYBE IT'S THE FLU.
HUH?

FOR A MOMENT I THINK HE MUST SURELY BE AN HALLUCINATION CAUSED BY THE BUG.
BUT THEN I REALIZE HE'S REAL. THAT GRACEFUL FORM CUTTING THROUGH THE MORNING SKY IS REALLY MY PAL, WARREN KENNETH WORTHINGTON III, A.K.A. THE ARCHANGEL.
X-FACTOR MUST BE BEATING THE BUSHES, TRYING TO FIND OUT WHAT'S HAPPENED TO ME.

I FRANTICALLY TEAR AT THE WINDOW TO CALL TO WARREN.
BUT THE BLOODY THING JAMS UP.
WHAT ARE YOU DOING?
IT'S MY FRIEND, WARREN...
WERE YOU GOING TO LEAVE WITHOUT SAYING GOODBYE?

YOU LOOK TIRED, HANK, TERRIBLY TIRED.
A LITTLE MORE REST IS WHAT YOU REALLY NEED.
HANK!
WHAT?!

IT CAN'T BE REAL!
IT CAN'T BE HAPPENING!
SYNTHIA'S EYES PLEAD FOR ME TO HELP.
WHAT THE DEVIL ARE YOU DOING?!
!
ANYTHING WE WANT!!

THAT TAKES CARE OF THAT OL' PARTY POOPER.
LET'S BOOGIE, BOSS MAN!

YOU KNOW, I DON'T LIKE YOUR LOOKS, BLONDIE.

I THINK I'LL CHANGE THEM. WHAT YA THINK ABOUT THAT?

BAD IDEA, SCOTT.

IN FACT, IT'S A TERRIBLE IDEA!

THE GANG GOES INTO ACTION, JUST THE WAY I'VE SEEN THEM DO IT A THOUSAND TIMES BEFORE.
THAT'S HOW I ANTICIPATE THEIR MOVES AND AVOID THEIR INITIAL ASSAULT.
MAYBE THIS IS REAL.

CAN IT BE THAT I'VE NEVER SEEN THEIR TRUE FACES BEFORE THIS MOMENT?
ARE MY EYES ONLY OPEN NOW FOR THE FIRST TIME?

THEY SAY LOVE CHANGES THE WHOLE WORLD FOR YOU.
MAKES YOU SEE IT DIFFERENTLY.

IF THAT'S TRUE, MY LOVE FOR SYNTHIA HAS REVEALED WHAT A NIGHTMARE EXISTENCE I'VE BEEN LIVING.

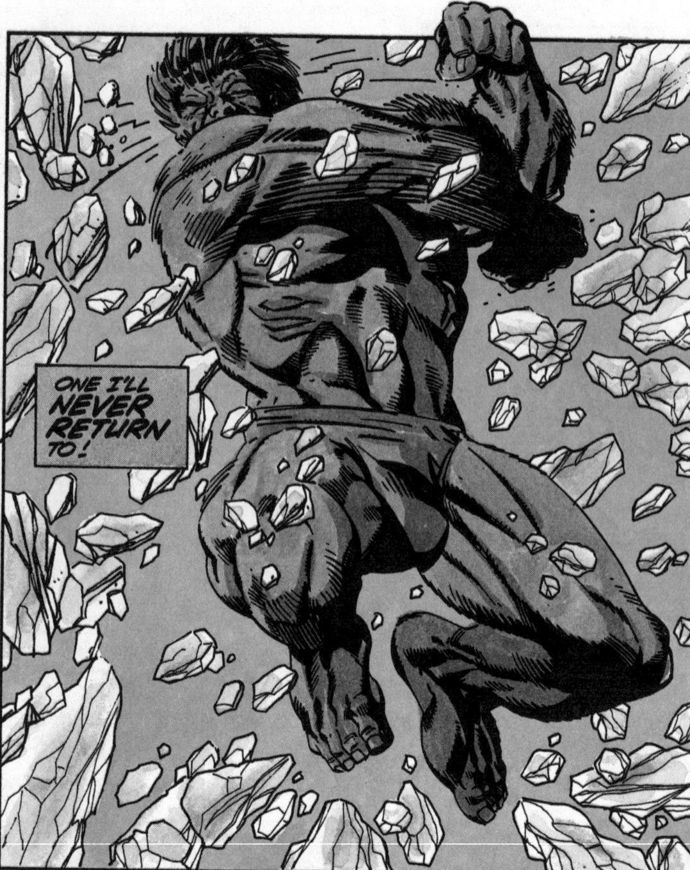
ONE I'LL NEVER RETURN TO!

SYNTHIA?
ARE YOU ALL RIGHT?
YES...

YOU SAVED ME.

"BUT I'M STILL YOUR PRISONER, AREN'T I?"
"AREN'T WE ALL PRISONERS TO SOMETHING?"

"I'M YOUR SLAVE AND THERE'S NOTHING I CAN DO TO BREAK THE CHAINS THAT BIND ME."
"BECAUSE YOU FIND THE CHAINS COMFORTING. THEY ARE OF YOUR OWN MAKING."

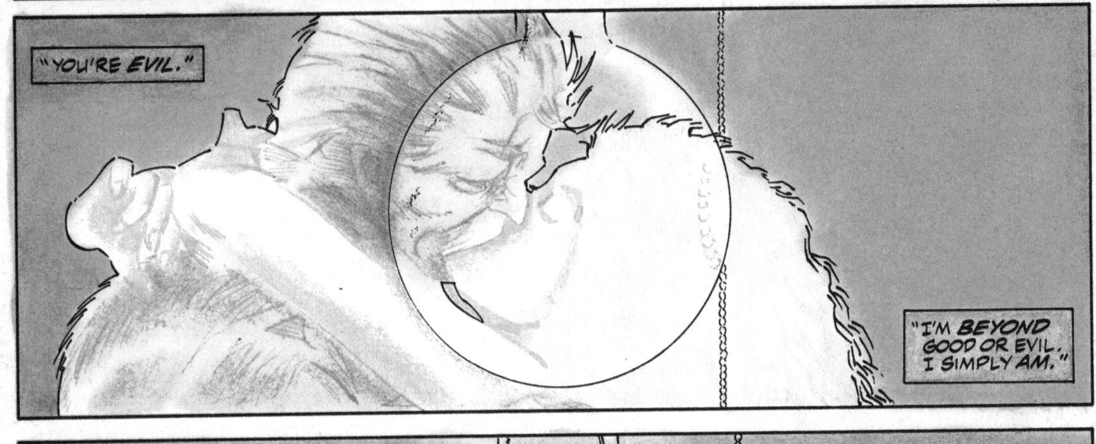
"YOU'RE EVIL."
"I'M BEYOND GOOD OR EVIL. I SIMPLY AM."

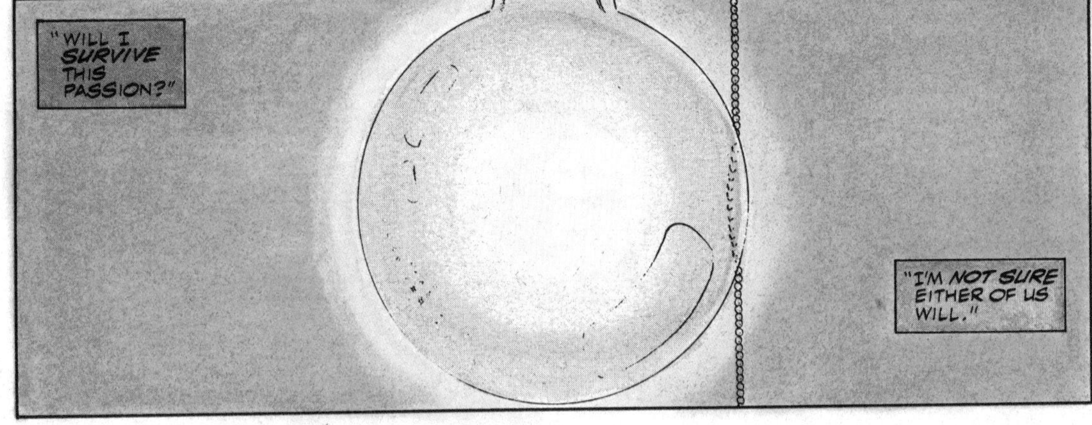
"WILL I SURVIVE THIS PASSION?"
"I'M NOT SURE EITHER OF US WILL."

I'M GETTING NEAR THE END OF MY ROPE.
BURNING OUT.
TOO WASTED TO EVEN MOVE.
SYNTHIA...
I'M DYING, SYNTHIA.
NO, YOU ONLY FEEL LIKE YOU ARE.
REMEMBER, I WARNED YOU HOW IT WOULD BE.
IT'S ALL FEELINGS, NOTHING BUT FEELINGS.

WHY, SYNTHIA? WHY DOES IT HAVE TO BE LIKE THIS?
POOR BEASTY, ALL CONFUSED.
YOU SAID YOU'D EXPLAIN...
AND PERHAPS I SHOULD.
AFTER ALL, THE TIME FOR YOU TO PLAY THE KNIGHT IN SHINING ARMOR IS ALMOST UPON US.
WHAT ARE YOU?
SOMETHING YOU COULDN'T EVEN BEGIN TO COMPREHEND.
ONCE THE COSMOS WAS FILLED WITH MY KIND. OUR NUMBERS SEEMED INFINITE.
BUT THEN THEY CAME.
THEY?
THE ENEMY.
THOSE THAT SEEK TO ANNIHILATE US. THE DARK ONES.
THEY FEAR AND HATE OUR LIGHT AND PLEASURE.
BUT THEY HAVE THE POWER TO EXTINGUISH BOTH.
NOW THERE ARE SO FEW OF US AND SO MANY OF THEM.
THE DARK ONES GROW EVER STRONGER.

ONE OF THEM NOW STALKS *ME*.
THE *DARK ONE!*
AS SO YOU PERCEIVE HIM.

HE'LL BE HERE SOON AND I HAVE *NO HOPE* OF DEFEATING HIM *ALONE*.
I NEED *YOUR HELP!*

I AM EXTREMELY *WEAK* FROM FLEEING THIS TERROR.
THAT IS WHY I HAVE BEEN *HIDING* ON THIS BACKWASH WORLD, TRYING TO *REGAIN* MY *STRENGTH*.

IT HAS BEEN DIFFICULT BECAUSE I HAD TO *CAREFULLY CHOOSE* WHOSE ENERGIES I *STOLE*.

I ONLY *TAPPED* INTO THOSE WHO WOULD *SIDE* WITH THE DARK ONES.

BUT THEN *YOU* CAME ALONG.

YOU WERE SO ASTONISHINGLY *DIFFERENT*.

WHEN I FIRST ARRIVED I KEYED INTO THE *HUMAN FACTOR* BECAUSE I THOUGHT THEM THIS WORLD'S *DOMINANT SPECIES*.
I KNEW *NOTHING* OF MUTANTS...

...UNTIL YOU SHOWED UP IN THAT *ALLEY*.
YOUR ARRIVAL *TRULY SURPRISED* ME.

I DIDN'T *SENSE* YOUR PRESENCE BECAUSE YOU AREN'T *TRULY HUMAN*.
I DOUBT THE *DARK ONE* WILL BE ABLE TO SENSE YOU EITHER.

A SURPRISE ATTACK FROM YOU MIGHT DO THE TRICK...
...GET HIM TO LOWER HIS GUARD ENOUGH FOR ME TO SLIP PAST IT.
IT'S THE ONLY HOPE I HAVE. PLEASE, HELP ME.
FOR YOU... ANYTHING!

THEN YOU MUST LISTEN CAREFULLY TO WHAT I SAY.
AN ENCOUNTER BETWEEN BEINGS OF OUR ILK IS LIKE NOTHING YOU HAVE EVER EXPERIENCED. IT WILL BE DISORIENTING.

YOU MUST STAND BY THIS WALL AND CLOSE YOUR EYES VERY TIGHTLY.
DO NOT OPEN THEM UNTIL YOU HEAR ME ADDRESS THE DARK ONE.

THEN LOOK ONLY AT THE DARK ONE. CONCENTRATE ON NOTHING BUT HIM.
IF YOU ALLOW YOUR EYES TO STRAY, VERTIGO WILL OVERCOME YOU.

IF THAT HAPPENS, ALL IS LOST FOR BOTH OF US.
DO YOU UNDERSTAND WHAT I'M SAYING?
YES... BUT I'M... SO WEAK...

DO NOT WORRY ABOUT THAT FOR THE MOMENT.
YOU MUST HOLD YOUR ATTACK UNTIL YOU HEAR ME SCREAM THE WORD "NOW!"

WHAT ABOUT YOU?
I WILL BE WITH YOU, FIGHTING ALONGSIDE YOU.

I SHALL ALWAYS BE BY YOUR SIDE IN MY OWN FASHION.
HER KISS...

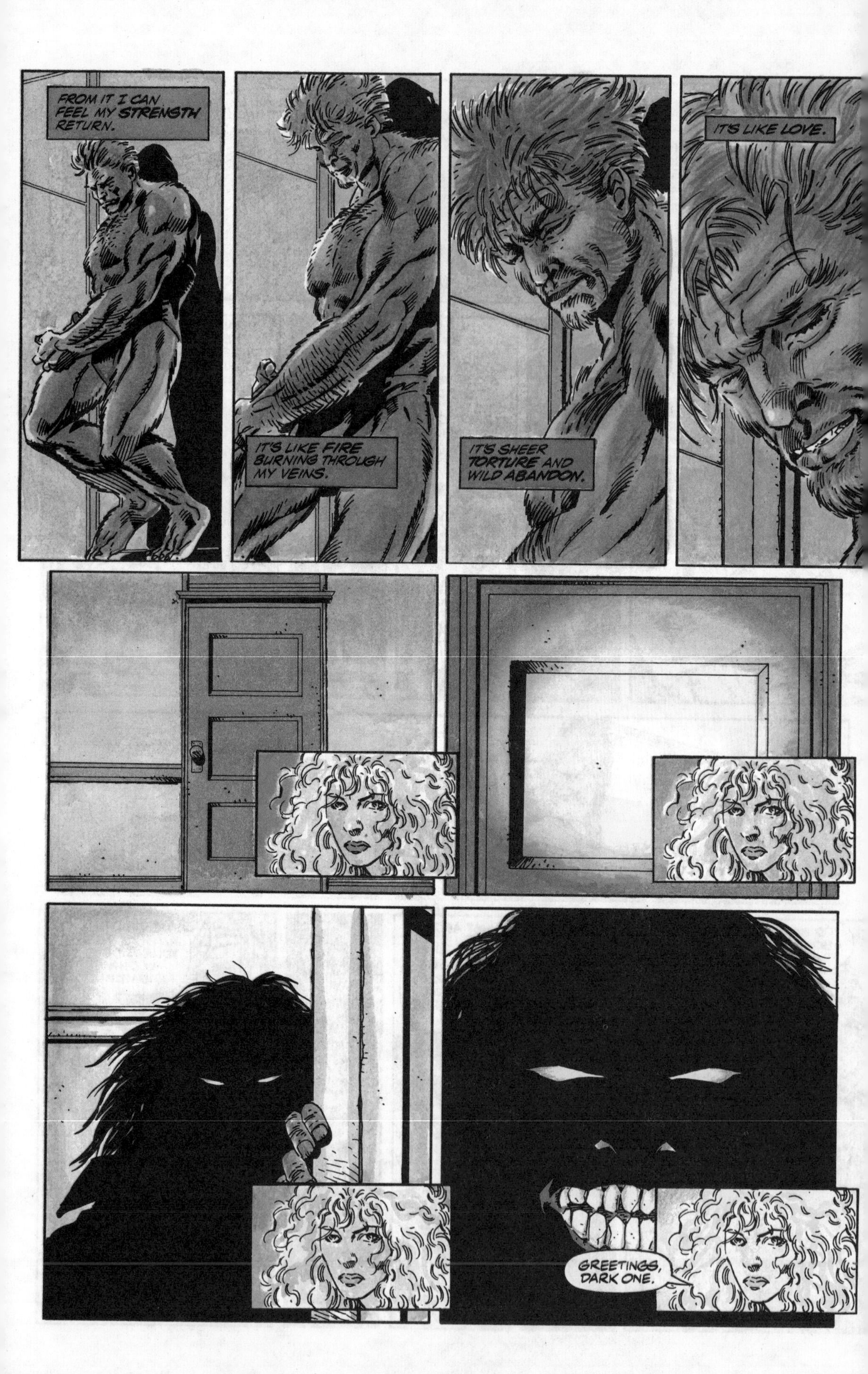
FROM IT I CAN FEEL MY STRENGTH RETURN.
IT'S LIKE FIRE BURNING THROUGH MY VEINS.
IT'S SHEER TORTURE AND WILD ABANDON.
IT'S LIKE LOVE.
GREETINGS, DARK ONE.

BLAST YOU, SYNTHIA! WHY DIDN'T YOU WARN ME IT'D BE LIKE THIS!
ALWAYS PLAYING GAMES! ALWAYS KEEPING ME IN THE DARK! BLAST YOU!
THE APARTMENT, REALITY, EVERYTHING'S MELTING AWAY TO AN INTERDI-MENSIONAL SMOR-GASBORD OF EVER-SHIFTING ACTUALITIES.
MY STOMACH BREAKS INTO AN INSANE TARANTELLA, THREATENING TO REVOLT.
BUT SOMEHOW I HOLD IT TOGETHER AND REMEMBER SYNTHIA'S WORDS.
"LOOK ONLY AT THE DARK ONE!"

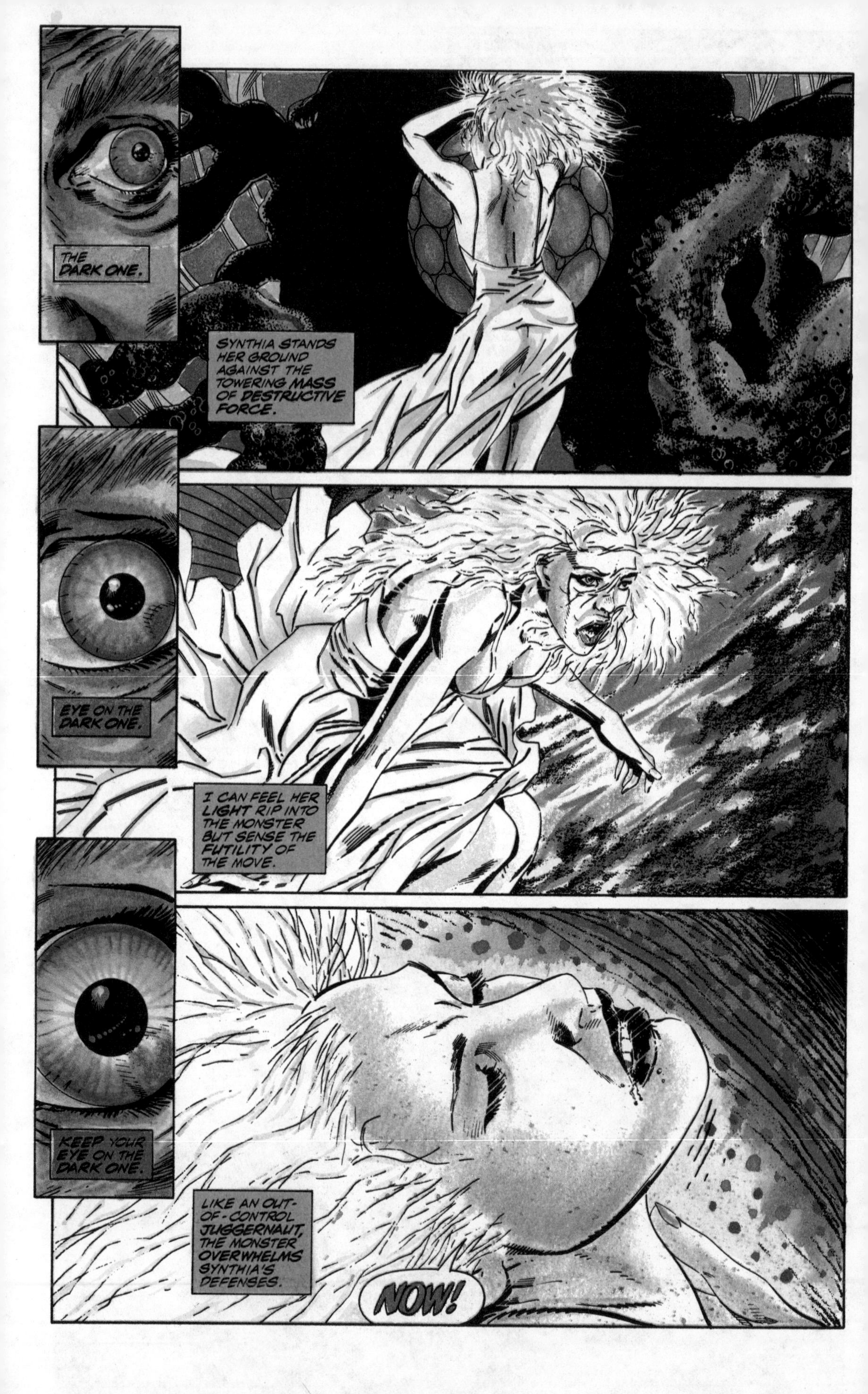
THE DARK ONE.
SYNTHIA STANDS HER GROUND AGAINST THE TOWERING MASS OF DESTRUCTIVE FORCE.
EYE ON THE DARK ONE.
I CAN FEEL HER LIGHT RIP INTO THE MONSTER BUT SENSE THE FUTILITY OF THE MOVE.
KEEP YOUR EYE ON THE DARK ONE.
LIKE AN OUT-OF-CONTROL JUGGERNAUT, THE MONSTER OVERWHELMS SYNTHIA'S DEFENSES.
NOW!

A MAD HOWL, FILLED WITH A LIFETIME OF ANGER AND FRUSTRATION, ERUPTS FROM WITHIN ME...

...AND DEATH TAKES NOTE OF MY PRESENCE.

BUT IT'S ONLY A FLEETING GLANCE, TERMINATED BY THE WORLD EXPLODING ABOUT US.

I'VE NEVER BEFORE FELT SUCH NAKED POWER RE-LEASED IN SUCH A DEVASTATING DISPLAY.
AND DEEP WITHIN THE HEART OF THE FIERY CATACLYSM I CATCH JUST A GLIMPSE OF...
SYNTHIA?!

...IS... IS THAT YOU?
YES, HANK, MY DEAR, IT IS ME.
YOU'RE... BEAUTIFUL...
AND SO ARE YOU.

ONCE AGAIN YOU HAVE SAVED ME AND FOR THAT I WILL ALWAYS BE GRATEFUL.
TO PROVE THAT GRATITUDE TO BID YOU FAREWELL.
"RETURN TO YOUR LIFE AND PROSPER."
SYNTHIA... WAIT...
DON'T GO... PLEASE...

HUH?
YOU GET MUGGED OR SOMETHING, MISTER?
SYNTHIA.
FROM THE KID I LEARN IT'S MONDAY, THE SAME DAY I TOOK MY LITTLE WALK.
HE DOESN'T REMEMBER ANY BLOND WOMAN OR STREET GANG AND THE EXPRESSION IN HIS EYES SHOWS HE THINKS ME SOME KIND OF HEADCASE.

I DON'T TRY STOPPING HIM WHEN HE MAKES UP A LAME EXCUSE ABOUT HEARING HIS MOTHER CALLING.
HE COULDN'T ANSWER THE ONE QUES-TION THAT REALLY NEEDS ANSWERING.
WAS SYNTHIA NOTHING MORE THAN A HALLUCINATION CAUSED BY A BAD HOT DOG?

OR DID I REALLY MEET AND FALL FOR THE MOST FANTASTIC WOMAN THAT'S EVER EXISTED?
FACT OR FANTASY?
NO CHANCE I'LL EVER BE ABLE TO TRACK DOWN HER APARTMENT OR TRACE HER.

FACE IT, McCOY. THERE'S NO WAY TO TELL IF ANY OF WHAT YOU EXPERIENCED WAS REAL.
CAUTIO
PROPERTY OF N.Y.
DEPT. OF TRANS

DID I REALLY LIVE OUT AN UNBELIEVABLE ENCOUNTER?
OR WILL I FOREVER ACHE FOR A PHANTOM MEMORY?

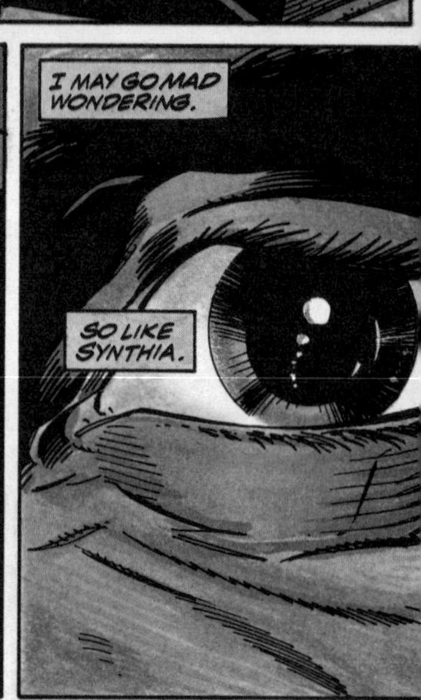
I MAY GO MAD WONDERING.
SO LIKE SYNTHIA.

THEN I FEEL IT.

IT'S THERE JUST UNDER THE FUR.
THE GOSSAMER TRACE OF TEETH MARKS ON MY HAND.

THE END